For Richard

Judy Moody
and the
NOT Bummer Summer

∾

Megan McDonald

**All photographs by
Suzanne Tenner**

SCHOLASTIC INC.
New York Toronto London Auckland
Sydney Mexico City New Delhi Hong Kong

ISBN 978-0-545-40273-6

Copyright © 2011 by CBM Productions, LLC.
Based on the theatrical motion picture *Judy Moody and the NOT Bummer Summer,* produced by Smokewood Entertainment Group, LLC. Text copyright © 2011 by Megan McDonald. Judy Moody font copyright © 2004 by Peter H. Reynolds. Judy Moody®. Judy Moody is a registered trademark of Candlewick Press, Inc. All rights reserved. Published by Scholastic Inc., 557 Broadway, New York, NY 10012, by arrangement with Candlewick Press. SCHOLASTIC and associated logos are trademarks and/or registered trademarks of Scholastic Inc.

12 11 10 9 8 7 6 5 4 3 2 1   11 12 13 14 15 16/0

Printed in the U.S.A.   40

First Scholastic printing, September 2011

This book was typeset in ITC Cheltenham.

Table of Contents

~

No More Snoresville
◠◡

L.D.O.S.! Last Day of School!

The countdown: only 27 minutes, 17 seconds, and 9 milliseconds until . . . SUMMER!

No more *S*-for-*Snoresville* summers. She, Judy Moody, was going to have the best summer ever. RARE!

Judy passed a note to Rocky before Mr. Todd came back.

To: Rocky, Frank, and Amy Namey
What: T.P. Club meeting
When: After school!
Where: Moody backyard: T.P. Club tent
Be there or be a SquarePants

Rocky flicked the note to Frank. Mr. Todd came into the room carrying a stack of papers. He had his **GOT MUSIC** cap on—backwards! He blinked the lights to get everyone's attention. Frank popped the note into his mouth.

"Pop quiz!" said Mr. Todd. Class 3T groaned.

"Just think: it's your *last* test on the *last* day of school."

"Aw! Nah-uh! Bad one!" everybody moaned.

"No way," said Frank. The note shot

out of his mouth and landed smack-dab in the middle of Rocky's desk. Slobber City!

"Gross!" yelled Rocky.

Mr. Todd passed out the quizzes. Mr. Todd cleared his throat. "Question number one: How many times did I wear a purple tie to school this year?"

Everybody shouted answers.

"Ten!"

"Twenty-seven!"

"One hundred!"

"Four!"

"Never!" called Jessica Finch.

"Never is correct!" said Mr. Todd.

"Number two: How long did it take our class to go around the world?"

"Eight days!" said Frank.

"Eight *and a half* days," said Judy.

"Too easy. Let's skip ahead. Here's one. This is big. Really big. We're talking MUCHO GRANDE!"

"Tell us!" everybody shouted.

"Can anyone—that means YOU, Class 3T—guess what I, your teacher, Mr. Todd, will be doing THIS SUMMER?"

"Working at the Pickle Barrel Deli?" asked Hunter. "I saw you there."

"That was last summer," said Mr. Todd. "But this summer, if you find me, you win a prize."

"We need a clue," said Judy. "Give us a clue."

"Clue! Clue! Clue! Clue! Clue!" yelled the class.

"Okay, okay. Let me think. The clue is . . . COLD." Mr. Todd hugged himself, pretending to shiver. "Brrr."

Jackson waved his hand. "Refrigerator salesperson!"

"Snow-remover guy!" said Jordan.

"Polar-bear tamer!" said Anya.

Judy thought and thought. Her eyes landed on the Antarctica poster tacked to the bulletin board.

"Ooh! Ooh! I got it! You're going to Antarctica. The real one."

"No, no, nope, and nope," said Mr. Todd.

Brring! Just then the final bell rang. Class 3T went wild.

"See you next year," said Mr. Todd.

"Unless we see you this summer!" some of the kids yelled.

"Bye, Mr. Todd," Judy called, zooming out the door. "Stay warm."

"Stay Judy!" Mr. Todd called after her.

Funk-a-delic

∞

"Last one in the tent is a rotten tomato!" Judy, Rocky, and Amy pushed past Frank into the T.P. Club tent in Judy's backyard.

"Hey! No fair!" said Frank.

Judy pulled out a giant, rolled-up poster board. "Okay, T.P.-ers! We are going to have the most way-rare, double-cool, NOT bummer summer ever."

"Time out," said Amy, making a T with her hands. "What's a T.P.-er?"

Judy, Frank, and Rocky stared at one another.

"We forgot!" said Rocky. "Amy's not even a member of our club."

"Yet," said Judy. "Quick. Frank. Go catch a toad."

"Me? *You* go catch a toad," said Frank.

"Why do we need a toad?" asked Amy. Everybody cracked up.

"You'll see," said Frank.

"You'll see," said Rocky.

"What about Toady?" Frank asked.

Of course! Judy was back in a flash from Stink's room, holding Toady, the club mascot, in her hand. She passed it lightning-fast to Amy.

Amy peered at the toad in her hand. "I don't get it. What's supposed to happen? If he jumps in my face, you guys are so dead."

"Just wait," said Judy.

"Just wait," said Rocky.

"Do you feel anything?" asked Frank.

"Yeah. A big, fat, slimy—" All of a sudden, Amy made a face as something started to drip from her hands.

"EEUWW!" she said, peering at the teeny puddle of yellow. She gave Toady back to Judy.

"Toad pee!" yelled Rocky and Frank at the same time. Judy, Rocky, and Frank fell over laughing.

"No way. OOH! Sick!" said Amy, wiping her hand on Judy's legs.

"Sick-*awesome*," said Judy.

"Now you're a member of our club," said Frank. "The TOAD PEE club."

"That makes you TOADally cool!" said Rocky.

Judy popped the rubber band off of her chart. "So, are you guys ready for my uber-awesome plan? Intro-DUCE-ing . . .

the one and only . . . Judy Moody Mega-Rare NOT-Bummer-Summer Dare." Judy unrolled her chart. "Ta-da!" Stickers and glitter went flying. "See? Thrill Points, Dare Points, Bonus Points, Loser points, and Big Fat Total."

"Huh?" said Rocky. "I don't get it."

"You know how summer's always Boring-with-a-capital-*B*? Thrill points are going to save summer. I spent two days and sixteen erasers figuring it out."

"Ride the Scream Monster? Surf a wave? Are these the dares?" Amy asked.

"Yep. See, a dare is something *way* fun that we've never done before and that we're kind of scared to do. Cool beans, huh?"

"Oh, boy," Rocky said. "I think I forgot to tell you some—"

Judy stuck her hand over his mouth.

"As I was saying . . . for each dare, we get ten thrill points. Plus bonus points if we do something crazy, like ride the Scream Monster with no hands. OR loser points if we chicken out."

"Ooh! And at the end of summer, we add up all the points?" Frank asked.

"Yeah. If we reach one hundred, then, presto-whammo, we just had the best summer ever. Is that thrill-a-delic, or what?"

Rocky looked green around the edges. Amy looked like she had just swallowed a frog. "Rocky forgot to tell you . . . he's going away this summer. To circus camp."

"WHAT?"

"She's going away, too," said Rocky. "To Borneo!"

Judy cracked up. "You guys! You

10

got me. I thought you were serious. Borneo. That's a good one. What even IS Borneo?"

"It's an island. In Indonesia. And I am going, for real, with my mom. We leave next Friday."

"Same here," said Rocky. "I'm going to learn to walk a tightrope and do magic tricks and stuff."

"That is SO not fair! How am I gonna have the best summer EVER if you're not even *here*?"

Frank looked up from the chart. "Hel-lo! I'm not going anywhere. *We* can still have fun."

"Great. Just . . . great."

After her friends went home, Judy sat in the tent staring at her blank chart. Suddenly, it did not look one bit thrill-a-delic. It looked *funk*-a-delic. FLUNK-a-delic. "It's just you and me now, Toady. Another long, hot, boring summer."

Stink's head popped into the tent. "Help! Toady's gone. He escaped!"

"Chill out, Stinkerbell. He's right here. We needed him so Amy could be in the Toad Pee Club."

"Hey, no fair! You guys had a Toad Pee Club meeting without me?"

"Be glad you weren't here. It was the worst Toad Pee Club of all time."

"Somebody's in a mood," said Stink.

"You would be too if your best friends were going to circus camp and Borneo for the summer. Now I'm stuck here being Bored-e-o."

"Not me! I have big plans for summer. Big*foot* plans. I'm going to catch Bigfoot!"

"Stink, the only big foot around here is your two big stinky feet!"

"Haven't you heard? It's all over the news. There are Bigfoot sightings everywhere. He's way close. Yesterday, Riley Rottenberger told Webster and Webster told Sophie and Sophie told me that Riley saw Bigfoot *at the mall*!"

"Yeah, right. And you, Stink Moody, are going to catch him."

"Yep! You can help if you want."

Judy rolled her eyes. "I'd rather catch poison ivy."

This was going to be the boringest, snoringest summer ever. For sure and absolute positive.

Bored-e-o

A week later, even though Judy had promised herself she was never ever going to talk to Rocky again, she walked across the street with her bike to say good-bye. Rocky's mom and dad, aunts, uncles, and tons of cousins were giving him a send-off party with a big good-bye cake and lots of singing "For He's a Jolly Good Fellow."

Judy helped Rocky lug a big suitcase to the backseat of the car. Rocky gave it one final push with his butt.

"So you're not NOT gonna go to

circus camp, huh? Sure you don't want to change your mind?"

"Are you nuts?"

"But what if you hate circus camp?" Judy asked.

"What's to hate? Tightrope walking, juggling, sword swallowing, lion taming—"

"Elephant-poop scooping all day? Elephant poop weighs like two hundred tons. Plus, it smells worse than a corpse flower."

Rocky's mom tooted the horn. "Time to go, Rock."

"Bye! Don't forget to write! We'll miss you! Break a leg! *Buon viaggio!*" called his family.

Judy stepped back. Her smile started to quiver. "Bye."

"Bye," said Rocky.

She trotted alongside the car. "Remember, if camp is super-boring, you can always come home!"

Judy hopped on her bike and raced after the car. "Don't say I didn't warn you about the pooooooop!"

Rocky waved from the backseat until the car disappeared.

Judy biked straight to Amy Namey's house. When she got upstairs, Amy was jamming the last Nancy Drew book into her zebra-striped backpack. Judy flopped on Amy's bed, blowing a huge bubblegum bubble.

"So tell me again why you're going to Bored-e-o?"

"Born-e-o. My mom's going to write an article on this lost tribe called the Penan. They've lived in the rain forest since forever, but all their land is getting wrecked because loggers are cutting down all the trees."

"That sounds so way un-boring. I wish I could help save a lost tribe."

"Go ask your mom. Maybe she'll let you come, too!"

"I will! See ya," Judy called, zooming out the door. Two seconds later, she popped back into Amy's room. "But in case she says no, here's something to remember me by." Judy dug around in her pocket and came up with a red rubber band, a lucky stone, and half a Grouchy pencil.

"Here," she said, handing over the pencil. "Write me."

"Sweet," said Amy. "Write me back."

Judy pedaled home as fast as she could, singing, "Oh, Borneo, I long-e-o to visit you-e-o . . ." She jumped off her bike, letting it crash to the ground.

"Mom!" she called, bursting through the door. "I have a great idea! Mommm-mmm! Guess what? I figured out how to save summer."

"Save summer?" Mom said, dis-tracted. "I didn't know it was in trouble."

"Listen to this. Instead of going to Grandma Lou's—bor-ing!—let's go to UN-boring . . . Borneo!"

"Borneo? Judy, that's halfway around the world."

"So? It's got a rain forest. And lost tribes that need to get found!"

Stink came into the kitchen and headed for the fridge.

"Stink! Guess what-e-o! We're going to Borneo! But we need money-o. Let's have a yard sale! I'll sell my pizza-table collection. You can sell your World's Biggest Jawbreaker!"

Standing on his tiptoes, Stink pulled a bag of red berries from the freezer.

"No way. I'm busy. Are these cranberries?" Mom nodded. Stink zoomed out of the room with the bag of cranberries.

Judy looked down at her mood ring. Wait! It was N-O-T NOT on her finger. Great. Now she'd lost her mood ring, too.

She, Judy Moody, was in a mood. And she did not need a ring to prove it was a bad mood. The baddest.

The next week was bor-ing without her friends. And the week after that. Even Frank got to go to Ultimate Adventures Day Camp. All Judy got to do was camp out on her bottom bunk and read the ultimate adventures of Nancy Drew.

Then one day, on the Fourth of July to be exact, Mom had some news. Maybe it was super-duper GOOD news. Maybe she, Judy Moody, could declare independence from a BOR-ing summer! Judy ran down the steps.

Mom put a hand on Judy's shoulder. "Honey? I have something to tell you." Judy plopped down at the kitchen table. "That was Nana on the phone. She and Gramps are moving to a retirement community, remember? But Gramps hurt his back, and they need some help. So we won't be going to visit Grandma Lou."

Judy bounced up in her seat. "You mean . . . we're going to visit Nana and Gramps in California instead? Woo-hoo! That's *almost* as good as Borneo!"

Dad stood in the doorway, holding

a roller brush in one hand. He had a smudge of green paint on his face. "Did you tell her?"

"Not quite," Mom said, glancing at Judy.

Judy looked from one to the other, confused.

"Listen, Jelly Bean," said Dad, sliding in next to Judy. "Your Mom and I have to fly out to California to help your grandparents. You and Stink—"

Judy stared at him, her heart in her throat.

"—are staying here."

"What?" Judy gasped. "You're going to leave me? To die of starvation and boredom and Stink-dom?"

"But the good news is . . . Aunt Opal's coming!" Mom said cheerily.

"Aunt WHO?"

"My sister," said Dad. "You know your aunt Opal."

"I met her when I was, like, a baby. She could be a zombie, for all I know!"

Just then, Stink clomped into the room wearing an old green blanket stuck all over with leaves, twigs, and cranberries. "Do I look like a berry bush?"

"Ummm . . ." said Dad.

"You look like a beaver dam," said moody Judy.

"I'm trying to fake out Bigfoot."

"Oh, in that case, then definitely," said Dad. "Absolutely."

"Great!" Stink skipped out of the kitchen.

"So," Judy said, ticking off on her fingers. "I'm not going to Borneo. I'm not going to California. And I'm not even going to Grandma Lou's?"

Mom and Dad nodded.

"This is the way-worst, double-drat, down-in-the-dumps summer EVER!"

Judy ran up the stairs and into her room, slamming the door. She flung herself onto her lower bunk.

"ROAR!"

Tingalinga, ding! Ding! Ding! Outside, the happy tune of the ice-cream truck drifted through the window.

Stink called up the stairs. "Ju-dy! It's the ice-cream truck!

Judy yelled back. "I am so NOT in the mood!" She rolled over and landed on something.

"Ow." Pulling out the Magic 8 Ball, Judy asked a question, shaking it hard: "Dear Magic 8 Ball: Could this summer get any worse?"

The window cleared: WITHOUT A DOUBT.

Aunt Awful

A couple days later, Judy was on her top bunk reading Nancy Drew mystery #44 when she heard a *Honk! Honk!* from outside in the driveway.

Dad called up the stairs. "Stink! Judy! Aunt Opal's here!"

Judy scrambled down from her top bunk and ran to the window. Just like Nancy Drew, she cracked the curtain to spy on this Aunt Opal person.

All she could see was a pair of short

blue boots sticking out from under a giant suitcase. She dropped the curtain and ran to her computer.

Dear Amy,
Summer just got WAY worse. Aunt Awful has landed! Please come home ASAP. Or else send me a ticket to Borneo!

Judy paced around her room, talking to Mouse. "I bet she has warts, Mouse. And evil oogley eyes. And makes us eat fish guts for breakfast!" Mouse licked his lips.

Bam! Bam! Bam! Stink stuck his head in Judy's room. "Mom wants us down-stairs. Now. To meet Aunt Opal."

Judy pointed to the sign on the door. "Can't anybody read around here?"

Stink read aloud: "'Do not disturb. Judy Moody is spending the summer in her room.' Really? The whole summer? What about food?"

Judy pointed to her window. "I have a basket. And a long rope. You can put food inside and I'll pull it up."

"What about TV?"

Judy held up a contraption made out of tin cans, toilet-paper rolls, duct tape, and mirrors. "What do you think this periscope is for?"

"Cool! What about going to the bathroom?"

Just then, a plume of black smoke wafted up the stairs. Judy heard a shriek, then a loud clatter and Mom's voice. "Oh, no! Dinner's on . . . FIRE!"

BEEEEEEP! The smoke alarm blared through the house. Stink raced out of the room. Judy grabbed her dolphin water pistol and ran for the stairs.

"Fire! Where's the fire? Help is on the way! Let me!"

Judy clattered down the stairs, her water pistol in one hand and a squirt toy in the other. Blazing into the smoky kitchen, she blasted water right, left, and center, hitting chairs, tables, Stink, Mouse, Jaws, and the smoky casserole that Mom was putting on the counter.

"Stop, Judy. It's okay—STOP!" Mom said.

One final blast of the squirt gun hit Aunt Opal, right between the eyes.

"Oops."

Aunt Opal shook her long red hair and laughed. "Judy!" Judy was instantly squished into a big bear hug.

"You've been here five minutes, Opal,

and already the house is on fire!" said Dad, opening a window. Mom flapped a dishcloth over the black casserole.

"Let me look at you," Aunt Opal said to Judy. "How old are you now? Twelve?"

"Nine. And some quarters."

Judy eyed her aunt up and down, from her hippie shirt to her bright blue boots to her arms jangling with bangles and bracelets. "Wow. You've got more bracelets than Chloe, my math tutor, and she's in COLLEGE!"

Opal twisted a braided bracelet off her wrist and handed it to Judy. "Here you go. This one's made from yak hair."

"RARE!" said Judy.

"I bought it from a monkey in Nepal for five hundred rupees. I think I got ripped off!" Opal rummaged through a large bag. "Here's your REAL present."

She handed a small box to Judy and a book to Stink.

"For me? Awesome!" said Stink.

Judy flipped open the box. Inside was the mother of all mood rings—a silver snake that curled around a glowing mood crystal.

"A mood ring! How did you know?"

Opal winked. Judy slipped the ring on her finger. It turned bright blue. "Blue is for *Happy, Glad*," said Judy.

Stink opened his book. "*So You Want to Catch Bigfoot?* Man, oh man, oh man, oh MANNN!"

"I think you're a hit, Ope," said Dad, putting an arm around her shoulder.

"I hate to interrupt, but what are we going to do for dinner?" Mom asked.

Judy and Stink didn't miss a beat. "Pizza! Pizza!"

* * *

Before you could say *pepperoni,* Judy and Stink were racing past China (Speed Bump #1) and past Japan (Speed Bump #2) on their way to Gino's Pizza.

"Let's go to Fur and Fangs while we wait," Stink said. "I gotta show Zeke, from my Bigfoot club, the new book. And prove to YOU that Bigfoot exists."

"Righhht." Judy rolled her eyes as Stink ran next door into Fur & Fangs. He rushed up to a tall, skinny teenager with hair in his eyes, waving his book.

"Hey, Zeke! Check this out!"

Zeke blew hair out of his eyes and let out a whistle. "Whoa. Sweet. It's a first edition!" said Zeke, admiring the book.

Stink smiled proudly. "This is Judy. My sister. She doesn't believe in Bigfoot. Can you believe that?"

"Seriously?"

"Mega-total super-seriously," said Judy.

"Show her, Zeke. Show her the proof!"

"Do you think she can handle the *Cave*?" Zeke asked. Stink nodded.

"Follow me," Zeke told Judy. He headed to the back of the store, past a red macaw on a perch. "Bigfoot lives! Bigfoot lives!" said the macaw.

Judy jumped, then quickly followed Zeke and Stink through a beaded curtain, past piles of cages, pet food, and pet supplies. Zeke's head bumped a BIGFOOT BELIEVERS sign as he ducked into a large "cave" made of old boxes and covered with spray-painted dog-food bags.

"What is this, a clubhouse for bats?" Judy asked.

"Welcome to the headquarters of the Bigfoot Believers Association!"

"Is this cool, or WHAT?" Stink said proudly.

Zeke pointed to a map of Virginia studded with pushpins. "These are all sightings of Bigfoot around here. We've been tracking his every move, and he is DEFINITELY headed our way."

Stink snatched up a clump of gray hair lying on the table. "Holy Pluto! Is this what I think it is? As in *Bigfoot* hair?"

"Nah. Chinchilla," Zeke said, laughing. "I had to brush one out this morning. Never mind that. Let's get to the real proof. I keep it in cold storage." Zeke stepped over to a fridge in the corner.

"Wait. . . . Did you say *cold* storage?" Judy asked. "Do you by any chance know a Mr. Todd?"

"Nope. Never heard of him." Zeke opened the fridge. Very carefully, he took a photo out of a plastic pouch. "Here you go. A rare photo of Bigfoot. Look, but don't touch." He held the blurry black-and-white photo out to Judy.

Judy snorted. "Are you kidding? That's just some guy in a fuzzy sweater! He doesn't even have big feet!"

"You're cracked!" said Stink. "They gotta be size fifty-nine at least!"

Zeke slipped the photo back into the pouch. "If you need more proof, come to one of our meetings. Tuesdays at six."

Judy shook her head. "I'm busy on Tuesdays. From now till forever. C'mon, Stink. Pizza time." Judy put her arm around Stink, dragging him out.

"Catch ya later, little dude," Zeke called after him.

Stink turned and gave Zeke a happy thumbs-up.

Gross Grub Club

The Moodys ate pizza at the picnic table on their back deck, under twinkly white lights and paper lanterns that Opal had strung up everywhere.

"Nothing left but crusts," said Stink.

"And some tuna fish for Mouse," said Judy.

"Tuna-fish pizza is the best!" said Stink.

"I hope you saved room for dessert!" Opal called.

Mom and Dad eyed each other. "Stink, it's rude to read at the table," Mom said.

"But check this out. Page thirteen. Bigfoot's bed!" Stink held up his book.

Aunt Opal came back outside, carrying a platter of hot-dog chunks in one hand and a bowl of bubbly, burping, orange-colored glop in the other.

"Ta-da!" said Aunt Opal.

"What is it?" Judy and Stink asked at the same time.

"Tangerine fondue!" said Opal.

"None for us, thanks!" said Dad. "We have to finish packing."

"Hot dogs for dessert?" Judy asked, her mouth hanging open.

"It looks like Bigfoot barf," said Stink. Judy cracked up.

Opal stabbed a chunk of hot dog with a fork, dipped it in the glop, and popped it in her mouth. "Mmmm. I used to make this for your dad when we were kids."

Stink peered into the bowl. "Are those Froot Loops?"

"Uh-huh. Dig in, guys!"

"You first," Judy told her brother.

"But it's so . . . oogley-boogley!"

"This? This is nothing. When I was in Bali, I ate grilled cockroaches."

"GROSSSSS!" Judy and Stink yelled at the same time.

"Tell you what: if you BOTH take a bite, we can all be in the same club—the 'I Ate Something Gross' Club."

Stink and Judy look at each other, bug-eyed. "Just one bite? And we're in the Gross Grub Club?" Stink asked. "For real?"

"For real."

"Pass the hot dogs!" Judy said, grinning.

At bedtime, Aunt Opal sat next to Judy on the top bunk, painting Judy's toenails in a rainbow of colors. "So *then,* after the Peace Corps, I trekked across the Sahara and after that I moved to Bali. Where I lived until about a month ago." Aunt Opal waved a fancy fan to dry Judy's toes.

"MEGA-cool! Is that where belly dancing's from?"

"Bah-li, not belly." She laughed. "It's an island." Judy wiggled her toes. "So what's up for summer?"Aunt Opal asked. "Any exciting adventures I should know about?"

Judy twirled the new mood ring on her finger. "Well, I *was* gonna have the best summer ever, but my friends wrecked it."

Opal climbed under the covers of the bottom bunk. "I hate when that happens."

"Seriously! We were going to do all

these way-exciting dares and get thrill points. But Rocky's at circus camp and Amy went to Borneo."

Opal turned off the light. Moonlight flooded the room. Judy snuggled down in bed with Mouse on her stomach.

"I LOVE dares," Opal said between yawns. "In Kenya, someone once dared me to ride in an ostrich race."

"Did you win?"

"My ostrich won—without me! I fell off at the starting line," Opal said sleepily.

"You know what, Aunt Opal? You just gave me an idea."

Konkkk-shu. A light snore drifted up from the bottom bunk.

"I mean, what if we STILL did the dare chart, but made it into a race? Me, Rocky, Amy, and Frank?"

Konkkk-shu. More snores.

"We could each do our own dares and keep track of our points! First one to get to a hundred wi—"

KONKKKK-SHUUU!

Judy hung her head over the side of the bed. "Geez, Mouse, Aunt Opal snores louder than a blender."

Just then, Judy leaned over too far and fell off the bed. "Aghhhhhh!" She knocked into her desk chair, which tipped over a floor lamp, which crashed into a tower of all fifty-six classic Nancy Drews.

Stink came running. "What's going on?"

"Shhhhh! You'll wake Aunt Opal!"

They tiptoed over to the bottom bunk. Opal was sleeping like a baby. Judy gently pulled up her blanket.

"She slept through that?" Stink whispered. "Weird."

"Okay. Back to bed, Stink."

"Hey, I was just reading. . . . Did you know that Bigfoot is scared of just two things?"

"Enough already with the Big Feet!" Judy whispered as she pushed him out the door.

"But don't you want to know what they are? Guinea pigs and—

"—car horns!" he whispered as Judy shut the door on him.

She grabbed her computer and quietly tucked into the closet, plopping down on a heap of dirty laundry.

Dear Amy and Rocky (you too, Frank!),
UBER-RARE IDEA! Let's do a dare race, starting right NOW! First one to get 100 points WINS! What do you say?
Judy

Judy waited. She peeled off a Band-Aid. She picked at a scab, hoping she could save it for her scab collection.

Ding! An e-mail. From Rocky!

A dare race? I am in. Check out what I did today!

Judy clicked on a photo of Rocky in a leotard, walking on a tightrope high up in the air, holding a long pole.

Ten thrill points, for sure, don'tcha think? Gotta get some ZZZ's now—tomorrow is sword swallowing! Byeeeeee . . .

"Just you wait, Rocky Zang," Judy whispered. "Just. You. Wait."

Thrills and Spills

It was time. Time to say good-bye to Mom and Dad. The cab waited at the curb while everybody hugged a million and one times.

"Can you bring us back some California bubblegum?" Judy asked.

Dad ruffled Judy's hair. "Better yet— how about I chew some and stick it on the official Wall of Gum, in your honor?

"RARE! Promise?"

"Cross my heart." Judy's parents climbed into the cab.

"Can we have candy for breakfast?" Stink asked.

"No," Mom said. "Bye! Be good!"

Judy and Stink ran after the cab. "Call us every day, okay?"

"Can we have candy for lunch?"

"Bye! Byebyebyebyebye!"

The cab was gone. Stink's lip started to tremble. Aunt Opal put an arm around him.

Just then, Frank came running up the sidewalk. "Is it time?"

"It's time," said Judy. "Synchronize watches. As of 2:12 p.m., Thursday, July seventh, the thrill race is ON."

Frank bounced with excitement. "So what's the first dare?"

Judy waved the picture of Rocky on a tightrope in Frank's face. "This."

"We're going to dress in leotards?"

Judy grabbed the paper back. "NO. Don't you see? He's walking on a rope. A TIGHTrope? Above the ground? It's DEATH-DEFYING!"

"Ohhhhhhh . . . yeahhhhh!"

In no time, Judy and Frank stretched a thick rope from a large tree in the backyard over the creek to a tree in the woods. Judy tied it tight and gave it one more twang just to make sure. Perfecto!

Just then they heard a *bang.* Then a *clatter, thunk,* and *thud.* Stink. He emptied a wheelbarrow load of boards by the base of the tree.

"What do you think you're doing?" Judy asked.

"I'm building a trap for Bigfoot!" said Stink. "I'm gonna lure him here with peanut butter. Bigfoot LOVES

44

peanut butter—page fourteen of my book—then *boom!* A net will fall out of the tree and land on his head!"

"Not out of this tree. It's mine. I called it."

"You can't 'call' a tree," Stink said.

"Oh, yeah? Watch me. Mine." Judy tapped the tree, smiling smugly.

Stink tapped the tree back. "Mine."

"MINE!" Judy said, louder.

"MINE!" Stink wrapped his arms around the tree.

Judy wrapped her arms around Stink and tried to pry him off. "MINE!"

Frank tried to pry them *both* off. "Stop it, you guys!"

Tingalinga, ding! Ding! Ding! "Ice-cream truck!" yelled Stink.

Everyone tumbled to the ground. Stink raced out to the street. "I scream,

45

you scream, we all scream for Old King Kold ice cream. . . ."

Judy bear-hugged the tree. "Yay! It's mine!"

Frank took off after Stink. "Frank, where are you going?" Judy called.

"To get ice cream!"

"But now's our chance. Before Stink gets back! C'mon! What's more important? Ice cream or thrill points?"

"Oh, all right."

Judy stuck out her bare foot, and Frank cupped his hands. She put her other foot on the rope, grabbed the tree trunk, and . . .

"TA-DA!" said Judy. "Now the high-flying, death-defying Judy-a-Rini will cross, um, Niagara Falls! One slip, and she'll fall to her doom!"

Arms outstretched, Judy inched

across the rope. "Check it out! I'm doing it. I'm crossing the Crashing Cataracts of Niagara!" She wibble-wobbled.

"Whoaaaa!" yelled Frank.

"Don't worry! The great Judy-a-Rini will not fall—*aggh!*"

Frank had stepped onto the rope. "Get off, Frank! One. At. A. Time!"

Tingalinga, ding! Ding! Ding! "Hurry up! I wanna get ice cream!"

Judy picked up her pace. "Ten thrill points, if only I can finish—"

Just then, the rope jerked super hard. "Mosquitoes! Incoming!" yelled Frank.

Judy's arms windmilled wildly as Frank flailed at the air around his head. "Stop WOBBLING me!"

"I can't help it! There's a mosquito on my—ahhhhhh!"

Splash! Crash! Judy and Frank sat up,

spitting water. Judy was dripping in mud and plastered with wet leaves. Frank pulled a salamander out of his hair.

Stink waved a large ice cream in front of them. "Ha, ha, you missed it!"

Frank glared at Judy. "When we go to ride the Scream Monster, I am getting TEN ice creams!"

Puke Monster

On Saturday, Judy was waiting for Frank. His older sister, Maddy, was going to take them to Scaredevil Island. Pieces of colorful old dishes, plates, bowls, and cups were spread all over the back deck. She watched Aunt Opal smash an old teapot.

"Hey, can I smash something? I usually get in trouble when I break stuff! What are you making, anyway?"

"I'm not sure yet!"

HONK! HONK! BEEEEP! Frank and Maddy pulled up in a blue MINI Cooper with a racing stripe. "Hey, Judy!" Frank's sister called. "Ready to rock and roller coaster?"

"Scream MONSTERRRRRRR!" yelled Judy. "I hate to smash and run, but . . . bye, Aunt Opal."

"Scream a little scream for me!" Opal waved as Judy ran to the car.

Hopping inside, Judy got a mouthful of something poofy and pink. *Pff!* "What's with the clouds of pink stuff?" she asked, blowing it away from her face.

"It's my prom dress," said Maddy. "I have to take it to the cleaner's." Judy wrestled the dress, pushing it to one side.

"No way would I be caught dead

looking like a gigunda poof of pink cotton candy," said Judy.

"Speaking of cotton candy," said Frank, "what are we gonna eat first?"

"FIRST we go on the Tilt-a-Whirl," said Judy.

"AFTER we get ice cream, right?" said Frank.

"Right. And snow cones."

"And corn dogs. And gobs of gum."

"RARE! We'll be ready for the Scream Monster, for sure."

The car drove past the Frog Neck Lake Swim Club. Judy and Frank snapped their heads around. "STOP!" they both shouted.

Maddy slammed on the brakes, screeching to a halt.

"Are you thinking what I'm thinking?" Frank asked.

"MR. TODD!" they said at the exact same time. "Cold water!"

Judy and Frank zoomed inside. They searched in the pool, around the pool, under the lifeguard, at the food window, even inside the Little Loo Loo. P.U.!

Frank's head popped up from inside a giant bin of pool noodles.

"Frog! I was SURE he'd be in here."

"Don't worry. We'll find him. We have ALLLLL summer."

Judy and Frank craned their necks, staring up, up, up at the twisting, turning roller coaster. Screeches and screams filled the air.

"Super-cali-fragi-listic-expi-thrill-a-delic!" said Judy.

Frank's blue tongue hung out. He

was holding two double-scoop blue-raspberry ice-cream cones in one hand and a purple snow cone in the other. Sticking out of his back pockets were cotton candy and a corn-dog-on-a-stick. "Geez LOUISE! How many thrill points is that?" said Frank.

"Ten. Plus bonus points for NO HANDS!"

The ride glided to a stop. People staggered out of their seats, eyes glazed, hair gone haywire. Judy handed twelve tickets to a guy with a Mohawk haircut and a T-shirt that said **SURRENDER TO THE SCREAM**.

"No food on the ride, kid," said Mohawk Man, pointing to a trash basket.

"What? No way am I throwing this stuff out!"

"Then step outta line, mister."

Frank stepped out of the line. "Frank! We've been waiting for an hour!" said Judy, dragging him back. "Surrender the snow cone!"

"Are you cracked?" Frank took a giant bite and crunched on the ice.

"Seriously! We gotta earn thrill points! So far we have a big fat ZERO."

"Okay, okay!" As Judy ran for her seat, Frank hurried up and stuffed his face with one last bite of everything. *Munch! Crunch! Slurp!*

"FRANK!"

Frank dumped the rest of his stuff and jumped into the lead car beside Judy. *CLANK.* A bar came down, locking them into their seat.

"This is it!" Judy said.

"Thrill points here we come!" Frank yelled.

With a loud *whirrr,* the train of cars lurched forward, inching up the track.

"Hands up!" Judy told Frank. "Every second counts!"

Frank lifted his hands. He started to look a little woozy.

"I'm not so sure about this," he told Judy.

"Too late now," Judy yelled. The car slowed as it reached the tippy-top of the first big hill. "Because here we goooooOOOOOOO!"

Wheee! The coaster zoomed down the hill at lightning speed. Just before hitting the ground, it shot back up in the air, twisting and turning in a sickening somersault of spirals.

"Ahhhhhhh!" Judy screamed.

"AAAHHHHHHHHH!" Frank screamed louder, clutching his stomach.

Judy's hair whooshed straight up in the air. She laughed and turned to Frank. Her smile disappeared in a blink. Frank's face looked like a cartoon. It had turned green—as green as Shrek. Greener than the Hulk!

"No no no no NO! Frank Pearl, don't you . . . DAREEEEEEEEEE!"

All of a sudden, Frank gagged, then *BLUCK!* He spewed a spurting stream of chunky blue upchuck. Before you could say Scream Monster, she, Judy Moody, was covered in blue.

The Scream Monster had just become . . . the Puke Monster.

Judy slogged up the sidewalk to the front door. The screen door was locked. The TV blasted news about more local Bigfoot sightings. "Reporting live from the Fur and Fangs parking lot, this is Jess Higginbottom Clark, WH2O."

Ding ding ding ding ding! Judy pressed the doorbell with her elbow. "Stink, I can see you in there watching TV. Open the door!"

Stink dragged himself away from the TV. "Did you hear that? That was Herb and Rose Birnbaum, from my Bigfoot club. They saw him! They really—"

He flipped the latch and opened the door. His mouth dropped open. Judy was wearing a giant, frothy, pink prom dress. She held a hunk of the dress in one hand and a messy-looking plastic bag in the other.

57

"Judy!" Opal called from the kitchen. "Did you have fun?"

"She went to the PROM with Frank Pearl!" said Stink. He turned to Judy. "What's with the weirdo dress? *Did* you go to the prom with Frank Pearl?" Stink teased. "Ooh! I thought you were going to Scaredevil Island."

"Knock it off, Stinkbug. I'm. NOT. In. The. Mood."

"Oof. What's in the bag? Dead skunks? P.U.-ee!" He pinched his nose. "Smells worse than elephant poop."

"*You* smell worse than elephant poop." Judy pushed past him.

"Wait! What happened? For real?"

"Don't ask. Seriously. DON'T ASK!"

"Where's Judy?" Opal asked, coming down the hall.

"Don't ask," said Stink.

"What's that smell?" Opal said, sniffing the air.

"Double don't ask," said Stink.

Minutes later, just as Judy slid down into the bubbles in the bathtub, there was a knock on the door.

"Stink, I told you not to ask!" she yelled through the door.

"I'm not asking. I'm TELLING. I mean, I'm just saying—you got a postcard from Rocky."

Judy perked up. "That's different. Why didn't you say so? What's it say? Can you read it?"

"Sure." Stink cleared his throat. He started to read in a fake deep voice. "'Dear Judy. How are you? I am fi—'"

"Knock it off, Stinkerbell. Just read it like a normal person."

"You don't want me to sound like Rocky?"

"I don't want you to sound like Darth Vader trapped in a vacuum cleaner."

"Okay, okay. 'Dear Judy. How are you? I am fine. Guess what? I just learned how to saw someone in half!'"

Judy sat up, splashing water everywhere. "No fair! I want to saw someone in half. Like Frank *Pukehead* Pearl."

Stink kept reading. "'It was super way cool! We even get to be in a real circus—you have to come, okay? August seventh. JSYK (Just So You Know). I'm up to thirty-seven thrill points! How many do you have?'"

Judy sank farther and farther into the suds. "I'd like to saw YOU in half, Rocky Zang."

Blub, blub.

60

"And I haven't forgotten you, Frank Pearl."

Blub.

"Are you done scrubbing off Frank Pearl prom cooties yet? Because I'm going to an emergency Bigfoot meeting. Wanna come? It starts in fourteen minutes and thirty-seven seconds."

"Stink, you have Bigfoot *on the brain.*"

"Okay. But don't be asking for my autograph when I capture Bigfoot and get all famous!"

Goliath Glue

Judy stared at her thrill-point chart. It was already the middle of July, and her chart looked Baresville. As in half naked. No frills. No thrills. She picked up a strawberry-scented smelly marker. "Ten points for riding the Scream Monster, Mouse. Minus five for blue throw-up and five for the prom dress equals—"

Mouse meowed. "You're right, Mouse. A big fat doughnut." Judy was tracing and retracing a zero in the total points column when *KA-BOOM*—she heard a huge crash. She flew down the stairs and skidded to a stop just inside the living room.

"What happened? Did the roof fall in or something?"

"I just dropped this." Aunt Opal held up a shiny garbage-can lid as if it was an Egyptian treasure. "I can't decide if this is a shield, a hat, or a chariot wheel."

"Um, I hate to tell you, but I think it's the lid to the garbage."

"Well, sure, but what is it *really*? I mean, what does it want to become?"

"Maybe it wants to grow up and become a Dumpster." Judy cracked herself up. She went over to a giant trunk full of art supplies. "What's IN here, anyway?"

"It's my traveling art studio," Opal told Judy. "With all my tools and supplies, I can make anything from mobiles to murals."

"You're an artist?"

Opal chose a hunk of fabric, Goliath Glue, ribbons, and a hammer, and dropped them onto the couch beside the lid. "A guerrilla artist, actually."

"*Gorilla?* As in monkey?"

Opal shook her head. "As in secret. Under the radar. A guerrilla artist makes art out of everything and puts it everywhere."

"Cool beans. But why?"

Aunt Opal smiled. "It's fun. And creative. And daring. See, here's what I'm thinking. . . ." Opal whispered to Judy. A big grin spread over Judy's face.

For the next hour, Judy cut, glued, and

painted paper insects. Aunt Opal hammered, twisted, shaped, and shined her garbage-can lid.

"It's way cool making such a mess!" said Judy.

"That's what art is all about," said Opal.

Judy swirled a huge glob of Goliath Glue onto the garbage lid with her hand, then stuck a butterfly, dragonfly, and her favorite insect, the northeast beach tiger beetle, onto the lid.

"Ta-da!" Leaning on the table with one hand, she struck a pose, showing off her hat. *Boing!* Bugs sprang up and down on metal Slinkies.

"Fantastic! I TOLD you it was a hat." Opal held up her own hat, which was decked out with pottery shards, ribbons, colored glass, and sparkly gems.

"Now all we have to do is sneak over

to the library and put these on the library lions. But it has to be late at night, after dark, so nobody sees."

"That's ten thrill points, for sure!" Judy said.

The door banged and Stink burst into the room, excited. "Guess what! Zeke gave me homework. I have to look for Bigfoot scat!" He proudly held up tongs, plastic bags, and a small shovel.

"Are you sure he wasn't telling YOU to scat?" Judy joked.

"Zeke says you have to sniff for a really bad smell, which I'm super good at by the way, and look for dark stuff that looks like potting soil on flat rocks. Then you poke it to see if it has any leaves or berries in it. Which is why you never leave home without—"

Tingalinga, ding! Ding! Ding! "Ice-cream truck!" Stink dropped his stuff like a hot potato and zoomed out the door. Aunt Opal ran after him.

"Wait for me!" Judy started to run, but the whole table came with her. *Help!* Her hand was stuck fast to the table! She pulled. She pulled harder. "Hey! Somebody! My hand! It's stuck! I'M GOLIATH-GLUED TO THE TABLE!"

Aunt Opal rushed back in. "What! You're kidding, right?" Judy tried again to pry her hand off, but all it did was lift the table. Opal dashed into the kitchen.

"STINKER! BUY ME AN ICE CREAM!" Judy yelled out the front door.

Opal came back with olive oil, mayo, and a spatula.

"This is no time to make a sandwich," said Judy.

"Trust me," said Opal. She poured olive oil and glopped mayonnaise all over Judy's hand. Stink came back, slurping a rainbow-colored Popsicle.

"Where's mine?"

"I thought you were coming out. How was I supposed to know you glued yourself to a table? Want some?" Stink asked, holding out his Popsicle.

"An ABS Popsicle? Already-Been-Slobbered? Forget it."

"This won't take much longer. I promise," said Aunt Opal.

"Famous last words," Judy said. Forty-seven tries later, she slumped over.

"Well, we've tried warm water, a chisel, hand soap, laundry soap, dish soap, and Goo-B-Gone."

Aunt Opal jiggled Judy's arm. Judy wiggled, one, two, three fingers.

"Almost, almost . . . there!" Aunt Opal cried.

At last, Judy's hand flew up off the table.

"Free at last! In just under"—Stink checked the clock—"one hour and forty-seven minutes!"

"I had no idea that glue was so strong," said Opal. "How's your hand?"

"Better, now that there's no table stuck to it. I'm going to need some Band-Aids for sure. But my mood ring's in a bad mood. I think it's gonna be stuck on black forever. Ugh. This. Was the worst day. Of my life."

"Worse than the time I got to dress up as a human flag and go to the White House?" Stink asked. "And you had to go to school and dress up as a cavity?" Judy chased Stink around the table with the Goliath Glue bottle.

"Sorry, Judy," Aunt Opal said. "I'll make it up to you. Anything you want."

Judy looked at her. "Really? You mean it? Anything?"

Aunt Opal nodded. Judy slid the newspaper over. "While I was stuck, I saw this ad in the paper. Next Saturday, there's a Cemetery Creep 'n' Crawl after dark. Can we go?"

"Is it worth thrill points?" Aunt Opal asked.

"A *midnight* zombie walk? Through a graveyard? Did I say *midnight*?"

"Then totally. AbsoLUTEly."

Poop Picnic

Judy could hardly wait for the Creep 'n' Crawl! At last, it was Saturday. Aunt Opal was—*slap-dash*—making sandwiches and jamming them into plastic bags. Wearing rubber gloves, Stink was cramming scat samples into plastic bags. Judy sat in the corner, tapping out a one-handed e-mail with the UN-Band-Aided, NOT Goliath-Glued hand.

"So. We'll leave in a few minutes and eat our picnic at the cemetery, okay?" said Aunt Opal.

"RARE! Extra thrill points for eating with skeletons! I need 'em because— guess what?—Amy just went swimming with a shark!"

"Lemme see, lemme see, lemme see!" said Stink, throwing his scat bags on the counter.

Judy angled the computer so he could take a look. Stink read aloud.

"'Dear Judy Most Moody, Yesterday, I did the most sick-awesomest thing— I SWAM with a SHARK! That's like twenty thrill points, at LEAST!'"

Stink whistled. "Whoa! You're gonna lose this race SO bad. Hey, look. Your ring is GREEN! Green with ENVY!"

Judy looked down at her mood ring. Sure enough, it was pulsing green.

"Time to go!" Opal grabbed the picnic basket. Judy and Stink followed her.

"Your ring is green like POND SCUM! Green like BOOGERS!"

"Stink, you're a super-galactic booger." Judy and Stink stopped at the car. "Hey, Aunt Opal! Where are you going?" Judy called.

"To the cemetery! Aren't we walking?" Judy and Stink burst out laughing.

"No way. It's a million miles from here. We have to take Humphrey."

"Who's Humphrey?"

"That's what Dad calls our car. He says it looks like a Humphrey."

Aunt Opal smiled. "Your dad used to have a bike named Humphrey. Hey, I know! Let's ride bikes!"

Stink shook his head. "Not allowed. Not after dark."

Aunt Opal chewed her lip. "Bummer. Okay, then—here we go, I guess."

Judy and Stink buckled up in the back-seat. Opal put the car in gear, turned to look out the back, and lurched forward. She slammed on the brakes.

"Hey! Watch out!" Judy yelled.

"Um, you *do* know how to drive, right?" Stink asked.

"Of course! I drove across the Horn of Africa . . . about ten years ago." She shifted the car into reverse this time, then hit the gas. The car swerved wildly into the street, screeching and jerking to a stop.

"You call that driving?" Stink yelled.

"Sorry. No worries. It's all coming back to me."

"Watch out! You're gonna hit the—"

Humphrey bumped up onto the sidewalk.

"—mailbox."

"Holy . . . crap!" shouted Aunt Opal.

"Dear Magic 8 Ball: Could this summer get any worse?"

Judy Moody

Who's

Aunt Opal

(Jordana Beatty)

(Heather Graham)

Frank Pearl

Mouse

(Preston Bailey)

(Tails/Tux)

Mr. Todd

Mrs. Moody

Mr. Moody

(Jaleel White)

(Janet Varney)

(Kristoffer Winters)

Who

Stink
(Parris Mosteller)

Zeke
(Jackson Odell)

Mrs. Birnbaum
(Sharon Sachs)

Jessica Finch
(Ashley Boettcher)

Mr. Birnbaum
(Robert Costanzo)

Rocky Zang
(Garrett Ryan)

Amy Namey
(Taylar Hender)

A meeting of the "I Ate Something Gross" Club

This tree is MINE! I called it.

"Thrill points here we come!"

"I COME FOR DINNER. I COME FOR YOU-U-U-U-U!"

"Mr. Bigfoot? We come in peace!"

"I'm afraid we need this bike. It's an emergency."

"Do we have a volunteer from the audience?"

"Fifty cents to touch Bigfoot!"

"Aunt Opal!" Judy whispered urgently. . . . "Look! LOOK!"

"You said *crap*! *Crap*'s a swear!" Stink gasped.

"*Crap* is not a swear. Is there a map in this car? I have NO idea where I'm going."

Stink and Judy looked at each other with dread. Judy rustled around on the floor and found a map.

"Can you get a ticket for driving too slow?" Stink asked.

Aunt Opal hit the gas again. The map went flying—right out the window.

After driving around and around for what felt like hours, Judy pointed to the rusty old Ferris wheel at a boarded-up amusement park. "Hey, we already passed this place like three times," Judy said.

Splutter, splutter, splunk. Aunt Opal drifted into the cracked and grassy parking lot. "Uh-oh. We are Out. Of. Gas."

"Not to mention . . . Way. Super. Lost," said Stink.

Judy looked around. "Are we still even in Virginia?"

"Of course we're in Virginia. See that sign?" A dusty old sign dangled from a single chain: LARKSPUR PIER. VIRGINIA'S #1 TOURIST ATTRACTION.

"Can we eat? I'm starving," said Stink.

"I'm Judy," said Judy. "Pleased to meet you, Starving."

"Hardee-har-har," said Stink.

Flap! Down came the beach blanket onto a rickety, three-legged picnic table. Judy and Stink squished into a giant cup from the old teacup ride.

"Look at that," said Opal. "We're eating in the Fun Zone!"

"You mean the UN-Zone," said Judy. "It's missing a letter."

"This has gotta be worth some thrill points," said Opal, too cheerily.

"Not as much as a cemetery Creep 'n' Crawl."

Aunt Opal opened the picnic basket. "I know. Sorry 'bout that. Let's see, baloney for you . . . and turkey for Stink."

"But no mayo, right?" said Stink. "Mayo is gross-o."

Judy pulled out her sandwich and raised it to her mouth. JUST as she was about to chomp down, she sniffed her sandwich. "Something smells weird."

Stink took a whiff of his sandwich. "Mine smells funny, too. Almost like—"

Her teeth touched the bread. She was about to take a bite, when—

"SCAT!" Stink swatted the sandwich out of Judy's hand. He flipped it over. Stink jumped up and pointed. "Oogley-boogley, ugh, ugh, ugh!

Judy stared at something brown and squishy on the bottom of her sandwich. "What IS that?"

"It's scat! As in doo-doo! Dung! Manure! POOP!" He showed her his sandwich, smeared with brown goo.

Judy and Stink hopped up and leaped as far away as they could, falling off their giant tea cup and screaming "AGHHHHH!"

Aunt Opal slammed the basket cover on the rest of the bags. "Crap!"

"That too," Stink said, smiling.

A week later, Judy took her new post-card from Rocky up to her room. She taped it to Jaws, next to her laptop.

HAPPY NATIONAL HOT DOG DAY!
(If you get this on July 23.) I'm up to
60 POINTS!
—The Rock Man

Judy turned on her computer and started typing an e-mail.

Dear Rocky,
Sorry I haven't written in soooo long. You won't believe all the stuff that's happened in the last couple of weeks. Have you ever been on a poop picnic? I have and it STINKS on ice! Hardee-har-har.

Judy heard loud laughter coming from Stink's room. "Be quiet, you guys! I can't hear myself write!" She popped her head into Stink's room. He was giving Aunt Opal a driving lesson on his race-car bed. "So the main thing is, you hold your hands on the steering wheel at ten and two, like a clock."

"You guys are *driving* me crazy," said Judy. "Can't you play a *quiet* game like Sign Language or something?"

"Or something," said Stink. He hopped up and shut the door.

Judy went back to her letter.

We canNOT find Mr. Todd anywhere! Frank and I looked—at the mall, at the park, at Speedy Market. We even found a guy with a GOT MUSIC cap just like Mr. Todd's, but he turned out to be A STATUE!
Amy has a bazillion Borneo points. Get this: I'm almost out of dares and I still don't have ONE SINGLE thrill point!

No lie! I tried to ride an elephant at the zoo. But Aunt Opal wrecked the car on the way there and we got hauled away by a tow truck. Zero thrill points. One night last week we tried to sneak out after dark and do gorilla art. (Long story.) Bad idea. Rained out. Then there was the surfing lesson with Frank at the beach. Really, really bad idea. I ended up kissing a dead jellyfish! Bluck!

So my thrill point count is nada, zip, zero, zilch, thanks mostly to SpongeFrank SquareBottom! Please, please, PUH-LEASE think up some more dares for me because summer is more than half over and I'm gonna be a no-point, dare-doing loser!"

Frankenscreamer
∞

About a week later, Judy was pulling a torn and dirty wedding dress on over her shorts when the doorbell rang. "Judy! Frank's here!" called Aunt Opal. "Or should I say *Frankenstein's* here?"

Judy gave one last tug to the bee-hive fright wig on her head. "Coming!" She grabbed her backpack and raced downstairs.

"Hey, Judy! Ready for the Evil Creature Double Feature?"

"I love your square head," said Judy. "Are those real bolts in your neck?"

"Who are YOU?" asked Stink.

"Bride of Frankenstein. Who else?" said Judy.

"And I'm Frankenstein!" said Frank proudly.

"Of *corpse* you are!" Stink cracked himself up. "Oo-oh. Frank and Ju-dy, sitting in a tree! K-I-S-S-I-N-G."

Frank turned beet red as Judy clamped a hand over Stink's mouth. "Take it back or I'll feed you to Jaws," said Judy.

"G-N-I-S-S-I-K." Stink shot out of the room.

When Judy and Frank got to the movie theater that night, the sign said, A MIDSUMMER NIGHT'S SCREAM SUMMER

FESTIVAL! Creepy music piped over the loudspeakers. They handed their money to a vampire-faced ticket seller with blood-dripping fangs.

"I vant to take your money! Mu-wha, ha, ha!"

"Since when do vampires wear ski jackets?" Judy asked. "It's summer."

"Since it's freezing in here! The air conditioner went psycho."

Judy looked at Frank. Frank looked at Judy. "Did he say 'freezing'? As in cold?" she asked.

"MR. TODD!"

Once inside, they raced around the lobby, searching here, there, and everywhere. No Mr. Todd.

"I'll check the boys' bathroom," said Frank. He burst through the door. Judy busted in after him.

"Hey! GET OUT! No girls allowed!" Frank pushed Judy out the door.

She waited. "Well? Is he in there? Did you find him?"

"Nope. Just Count Dracula and a mutant lobster," Frank said. "I give up. Mr. Todd's probably training penguins at the North Pole or something."

"Or something," said Judy.

Judy and Frank got buckets of popcorn and headed up the stairs. The small theater was packed with popcorn-throwing, candy-chewing vampires and zombies. Judy and Frank sat in the front row, dead center.

"Remember, this is a double feature. So no being a wimpburger, Frank. We have to stay till the very end if we want to get points."

"Don't look at me. You're the one

who'll be screaming your pants off as soon as the lights go out."

Judy glanced at her mood ring. Amber. Amber was for *Nervous, Tense*.

Just then, the lights went out. A bloodcurdling scream filled the room. On the screen, a pack of zombies staggered toward a woman. Her party dress got snagged in a car door. She let out a spine-chilling scream.

Frank grabbed Judy's arm. "Alone, bad. Friend, good," he said in a Frankenstein voice. He chewed his popcorn extra-fast.

"GRRrrrrrrrr," the zombies moaned and groaned.

"AHHHHH!" the woman screamed again.

A zombie's eye fell out and rolled down the street.

"Holy eyeball!" yelled Frank.

"Good thing he's dead already," said Judy.

"SHHH!" said a zombie cheerleader behind them.

"It's true. The dead are among us," said a spooky voice. "They're taking over the town of Pittsylvania. Lock your doors. Bolt your windows."

Zombies marched through town, punching through walls and knocking down doors. One zombie ate something that looked like a human leg.

Frank gasped, spraying Judy with soda. "I, um, just remembered . . . I forgot to feed my goldfish." He stood up to go, spilling soda everywhere.

Judy pulled him back. "Sit. Down. Don't get all Franken-scared on me now.

This is our absolute last chance to earn thrill points!"

A zombie staggered. His milky eyes and blood-streaked face filled the screen. "I COME FOR DINNER. I COME FOR YOU-U-U-U-U!"

"AGhhhh!" Frank screamed. He jumped over Judy's legs, toppling her bucket of popcorn. "I'm outta here."

Judy grabbed his shirt. "You are so NOT leaving, Frankenstein!" Frank pulled away and *RIPPPPP!* She had half the shirt in her hands.

Frank ran up the aisle. Judy tore after him, catching up to him just outside the theater.

"You are dead, Frank Pearl!"

"No. Zombies are dead. I'm going home!"

Judy threw up her hands. "Great. Just

great. Rocky and Amy are having the Funnest Summer Ever and I'm stuck with Frankenscreamer!"

"Hey!" said Frank.

"Rocky and Amy wouldn't bail after two seconds of Zombie! Rocky and Amy wouldn't knock me off a tightrope! Rocky and Amy wouldn't puke all over me!"

Frank glared at Judy. "Look who's talking! All your stupid points and dares and charts—they suck the fun out of everything. You're nothing but one big wet . . . FUN SPONGE!" Frank stomped off down the street.

"Fun sponge?" Judy yelled after him. "Rocky and Amy wouldn't call me a fun sponge!"

Frank kept walking. He didn't look back. Judy cupped her hands to yell at him.

"Well, if I'm a fun sponge, then you, you're a big fat fun . . . MOP!"

Frank turned a corner and disappeared. Judy kicked at the sidewalk. She turned back toward the theater.

"Hold on there, Bridezilla. Where's your ticket?" said the ticket taker.

"Inside. In my backpack. Honest! I already paid! Ask the vampire." Judy pointed to the ticket booth, but it was empty. No vampire.

"Sorry. No ticket, no movie," said the ticket taker.

Judy spun on her heel and stomped away. She kicked a leaf. She kicked a stick. She kicked a rock all the way home. "Fun. Sponge. My. Elbow!" The rock tumbled down the street and stopped in front of her house.

"What the . . . ?"

In the middle of the front yard, a mountain of junk—tuna-fish cans, burlap bags, old carpet remnants, chicken wire, ropes, and pipes—had been made into a giant statue. BIGFOOT!

Aunt Opal was on a ladder, smearing plaster on Bigfoot's face. Stink was working on his two large feet. Aunt Opal waved.

"What. Is. THAT?" Judy asked.

"It's Bigfoot, of course," said Aunt Opal. "I guess I really am a 'gorilla' artist now."

"Wanna help?" Stink asked, grinning.

Judy trudged toward the front door. "I'd LOVE to. Only I can't because I'm going to spend the rest of this bummer summer *in my room*! I mean it this time."

"Look out. She's in a mood," Stink said to Aunt Opal.

"Am not!" She ran up the steps, letting the screen door slam behind her. Judy stepped on a postcard. She peeled it off her shoe. The postcard had a picture of Rocky making a lion jump through a hoop. It said,

85 thrill points!

"ROAR!" Judy ran up the stairs and flung herself onto her bed. She couldn't help noticing that her mood ring had turned dark blue. For *Unhappy, Mad.*

Tingalinga, ding! Ding! Ding! Late the next morning, Judy woke up to the jangling of the ice-cream truck. She covered her head with a pillow.

"Hey, Judy!" called Aunt Opal. "It's the ice-cream truck! Judyyyyyyy . . . !"

A few minutes later, Aunt Opal, with a grape Popsicle in hand, tapped lightly on Judy's door.

"Come back when school starts!" Judy called.

Opal pushed the door open a crack. "Sorry, but this'll be melted by then."

Judy didn't budge.

"You don't REALLY want to spend the rest of the summer in your room, do you?" Opal gently lifted the pillow off Judy's head.

"Why not? My summer is totally wrecked. For sure and absolute positive," Judy griped. "But I will take the Popsicle. Don't tell Mom."

"That bad, huh?"

"Ye-ah! Frank Pearl, my used-to-be-second-best-friend-but-now-he's-my-first-worst-enemy, called me a FUN SPONGE."

Aunt Opal couldn't help laughing a little. "That sounds BAD. *Are* you a fun sponge?"

Judy slurped her Popsicle. "No way! HE'S the sponge. It's HIS fault I can't get any thrill points!"

"Righhhht. Thrill Points."

"Well, they're important. You can't have a NOT bummer summer without them."

"Oh, absolutely. Duh. That's like the Numer-One Rule of summer," Aunt Opal agreed. "So, we just need to get you more thrill points. We still haven't put hats on those lions!"

SLURP, SLURP, SLURP.

"The hats got all ruined, remember?"

"Well, let's think of something else."

"But I've already thought of everything. For sure and absolute positive."

94

Just then, a loud voice bounced in through the window. "Testing, testing . . ."

Judy and Aunt Opal looked at each other. They scrambled over to the window. A NewsBeat van was parked at the curb. A lady announcer stood in front of the Bigfoot sculpture, interviewing Stink.

"And your name is . . . ?"

"James Moody. But everyone calls me Stink," Stink said, beaming.

"So, Stink, Bigfoot fever is sweeping the county with twenty-seven recent sightings nearby. Is that what inspired you to build a statue of Bigfoot?"

"Stink's on TV!" Judy screeched.

"Last one downstairs is a fuzzy pickle!" said Opal. They pounded down the stairs and out the door.

"People say Bigfoot isn't real. How do you answer that, Stink Moody?"

"He is *too* real. And I'm gonna catch him!"

"If you *do* catch him, Mr. Stink Moody, you'll be the most famous kid in—"

Judy jumped in front of the camera, sticking her arm around Stink. She grinned a big, wide, purple-Popsicle grin. "Don't forget me! I'm a Bigfooter, too!"

"You are?" Stink asked, stunned.

"It's Judy Moody, with a J. And a U-D-Y," Judy told the newscaster.

"Yes, uh-huh. Good luck, kids! We'll check in with you later! This is Jess Higginbottom Clark, WH20, live for NewsBeat."

"Hey, you two just might be on TV," Opal told them. "We'll have to watch the news tonight."

Stink turned to Judy. "Since when are you a Bigfooter?"

"Since one minute ago. I just had the biggest brainstorm ever. Catching Bigfoot's worth like a million thrill points. Summer's almost over, Stink. This is my *absolute last chance* to get points. If we catch Bigfoot, I might even win the race!"

"Huh?" said Stink.

"Never mind," said Judy. "Just. Tell. Me. Everything!"

Code Bigfoot

Judy and Stink sat in the Cave in the back of Fur & Fangs, waiting for the Bigfoot Believers meeting to begin. "One more thing," Stink told Judy. "Dogs always howl whenever they see Bigfoot. Page forty-two."

Just then, Zeke banged a gavel down on the table.

"Okay, Bigfooters. The Tuesday night meeting is officially called to order." Zeke turned to a retired couple. They were both wearing **BOWLING FOR BIGFOOT**

T-shirts and had cameras around their necks.

"Rose and Herb?"

"Present."

"Stink?"

"Present."

"New member?"

"Judy Moody. Present."

Judy whispered to Stink. "Where is everybody?"

"What do you mean? This is it. This is our club."

"Weirdness," said Judy.

"Rose? Do you have a report?" Zeke asked.

Rose stood and opened a large flow-ered flip pad. "Three new sightings! It's the most we've gotten in one week."

"Excellent!" said Zeke. "Give me the coordinates."

"One woman saw Bigfoot taking laundry off her line at fifty-seven Ashberry Road, about a mile east of the mall. Someone else saw something large and furry at the dump." Zeke stuck pins in a map as she called out the locations. "The third SWEARS he saw Bigfoot last night at the corner of Croaker and Jefferson."

Judy gasped. Stink jumped to his feet, toppling his chair. "CROAKER and JEFFERSON? That's where we live!" Stink shouted. Herb snapped a picture.

"Whoa! You two could conduct an all-night surveillance!" said Zeke. "Are you up for it?"

"You mean like a stakeout?" Stink asked. "With a tent and binoculars and emergency sirens and whistles and stuff?" Zeke nodded.

Judy and Stink high-fived each other. "Yes! All right! Thrill-o-RAMA!"

"Excellent. Herb and Rose? You're in charge of equipment."

Herb saluted smartly. "We've got all the right stuff out in the van."

Judy and Stink followed Herb and Rose out to their van in the parking lot.

"Do we get to use night-vision goggles?" Stink asked.

"Yes, sirree," said Herb. He opened the back of the van. "Camouflage netting, night-vision goggles, camcorder, whistles, thermos for coffee. . . ."

"Herb! They don't drink coffee," Rose chided.

"We did one time when we were waiting for Santa," Judy reported. "It was blucky." She stuck out her tongue.

"Okay, then," said Zeke. "Looks like

you're all set." He hopped onto a black Vespa and put on his helmet, ready to leave. *Vroom!* "Good luck, little dude. You, too, Moody girl! Call me if you see anything. Day or night."

"That's the lot," said Herb, handing over one last flashlight. "Remember, if you need backup, this van is at your service."

"August sixth, 8:13 p.m. The trap is set . . . and the Bigfoot stakeout has officially begun. This is Stink Moody, reporting live from the Moody backyard."

"Stink!" said Judy. "Say that we hung up thirty-eight peanut butter jars for Bigfoot bait. And that you're pretending to be a berry bush."

Stink panned the camera over to Judy, who was staggering around, wearing the night-vision goggles. "Hey! You look like Owl Girl or something!"

Judy tripped and stumbled. "These don't work. I can't see a thing!"

"That's because it's not all-the-way dark yet, Owl Girl."

Aunt Opal came outside, holding a baby monitor. "Aunt Opal! Wave to the camera!" Stink called.

Aunt Opal waved. "Stink, you make a *berry* nice bush."

"Hardee-har-har," said Stink.

"Okay, kids. Let's go over our plans. You two will stay in the tent."

"Check," said Stink.

"If you see or hear ANYthing, call me immediately on the walkie-talkie."

"Check," said Stink.

"Hey, that's Stink's old baby monitor!" Judy said.

"Whatev. Now, what's our secret signal?'

Stink held the button on the monitor. "Code red! Code red!" he yelled.

"Perfect. The minute I hear that, I'll be down in a flash to help."

"Your mood ring's orange!" said Stink. "That means you're scared."

"Nah-uh," said Judy. "But, Aunt Opal, what happens if you fall asleep and Bigfoot attacks us and we're half-eaten before you get downstairs?"

Stink scoffed. "He won't attack us. I've been practicing Bigfoot sign language." Stink placed his hand over his heart. "This means 'I am your friend.'"

Judy rubbed her stomach. "This means 'Your head was delicious.'"

"Nobody's going to get eaten," said

Aunt Opal. "Now, remember our vow." Aunt Opal, Judy, and Stink crossed their hearts and fist-bumped.

"We will NOT. Fall. ASLEEP!" they said all together.

A half hour later, the house was dark. The tent was dark. Judy and Stink were sprawled on top of their sleeping bags, fast asleep.

All of a sudden, the rattle of a garbage can startled Judy awake. She, Judy Moody, heard creepy sounds. A cat screeched. Gravel crunched.

She tried to nudge Stink awake. "Stink! Wake up! Something's out there!

"ZZZZZzzz!" Stink rolled over on his side.

"Code red. CODE RED!" Judy whispered

into the baby monitor. She pressed the button to listen. But all she could hear was Aunt Opal snoring!

Judy grabbed a large butterfly net and unzipped the tent. She poked her head out of the tent flap and looked through her night-vision goggles. Spooky! The world was neon green and dark black. Sure enough, moving across the lawn was an oddly shaped, fuzzy, glow-in-the-dark creature.

"Holy macaroni! It's . . . it's him! Code Bigfoot! CODE BIGFOOT!"

The fuzzy, green, luminous creature approached the tree, bumping into one peanut butter jar after another. "Hey! Ow! Ow! Ow!"

Judy leaped into action. Racing to the tree, she lunged forward and *SWOOSH!*

She slammed the butterfly net down over the creature's head!

"GOTCHA!"

"Aghhhhhhh!" All of a sudden, the hammock came down out of the tree, knocking Judy and the creature to the ground.

"Ahhhhhhh!" Judy yelled. The creature yelled, too.

"Bigfoot!" Stink called. Stink charged out of the tent, flashlight in one hand, monitor in the other. "CODE RED! CODE RED! CODE RED!" he called, rushing over to the tree in his bunny slippers.

Trapped under the net, beneath the tree, was a thrashing, kicking, yelling, two-headed monster. Stink flipped on the flashlight, grabbed a corner of the hammock, and yanked it back.

"Hey! Get off me!" said the monster.

Judy yanked off the night goggles. "Fraannnk?"

"Juuudy?"

"Bigfoot?" said Stink.

"What are you doing here, Frank?"

"I um, my dad took me back to the theater to pick up our backpacks, and I saw the house was dark, so I thought I'd just drop it off in your tent or something so you'd find it, only I bumped into a jar and then you hair-netted me!"

"Sorry. I thought you were Bigfoot," said Judy.

Stink bounced the beam back and forth between them. "Ha! You scared Judy's pants off, Frank!"

"Not," said Judy.

"Ya-huh! I HEARD you! You were screaming your HEAD off—"

All of a sudden, they heard a loud cracking noise, coming from the deep, dark woods. Stink looked at Judy, eyes wide. Judy looked at Stink.

"Bigfoot," Stink dared to whisper.

"No way. That was an owl."

Just then, an owl hooted. "THAT was an owl. Or Bigfoot pretending to BE an owl!" Stink said.

"Let's go!"

Judy and Stink grabbed their gear and bolted for the woods. "Are you coming, Frank?" Judy asked. "It's worth mega-mega-thrill points!"

"I, um, sure, I'd like to and everything, but um . . ." A car honked. "That's my Dad. Gotta go! Bye!"

Judy and Stink tiptoed across the backyard. They crept closer and closer to the tree line. At the edge of the woods, they stopped to listen.

"Maybe it was really WAS an owl, Stink."

"Nuh-uh. That was HIM. I know it. Bigfoot is famous for his owl sounds. Page forty-two." Judy and Stink craned their necks, peering into the darkness.

"You go first. I'll hold the light," said Judy.

"You go first. I'm filming," said Stink, turning on the camcorder.

"Okay, Scaredy-Pants. But stay close."

Stink clung to the back of Judy's pj's with one hand, filming with the other. They inched into the woods. Stink's costume hooked onto a tree and . . . *SNAP!*

"WHAT WAS THAT?" Stink whispered.

"Shhhhh! You'll scare Bigfoot!"

Judy and Stink tiptoed farther and farther into the gloom, taking shorter and shorter breaths. "Stop. Look. There!" She moved the light across a large patch of matted grass. "Is this some kind of bed or something?"

"Ye-ah. A Bigfoot bed. Page thirteen. This must be where he sleeps."

Judy swallowed hard. "Then wh-where is he?"

"Maybe he heard us coming. He's probably watching us right now." Stink touched his hand to his heart. "Mr. Bigfoot? We come in peace!"

The wind whistled through the trees.

"Hello? Can you hear me?" Stink tried again.

Suddenly, a furry creature swung from a tree branch, brushing Judy's head and bumping the camera.

"AHHHHHHHH!" Judy and Stink dropped everything and ran, screaming, out of the woods. They ran across the creek, over the lawn, up the back steps, through the kitchen, up the stairs, and straight into Judy's room.

SLAM! Their screaming didn't stop until they were both huddled under the covers on Judy's bottom bunk. Judy scooped up Mouse and held him tight.

The Chase Is On

"And then," Stink told Aunt Opal the next morning, "we got so scared, we ran out of the woods and all the way upstairs and I had a sleepover in Judy's room."

"Aunt Opal, you missed it! You slept through the whole thing."

"Good thing I filmed it," said Stink. "There! See? That's his bed!"

"Are you sure?" asked Opal. "It looks like woods to me."

"He was there—I know it! Ask Judy."

"All I know is I got a possum hairbrush and ZERO thrill points."

Aunt Opal smiled. "Well, don't give up, you two. It can take years to catch a monster."

"Years?" said Judy. "I need thrill points A-S-A-P, as in N-O-W." All of a sudden, Judy stared out the window. Dogs started barking and howling.

Right there, before her very own eyes, in front of her very own house, a tall, furry gorilla creature with enormous feet dashed down the sidewalk! A pack of howling dogs nipped at his heels.

"Code Bigfoot!" yelled Stink. "After him!"

In a blur they all scrambled for the door. "After him! Go-go-go-go-go!" Judy yelled. Judy, Stink, and Opal tore down the street after him.

Bigfoot and the dogs turned the corner. "We have to catch him before he gets to Main Street! Cars will drive him cuckoo! Page twelve!" Stink shouted.

Tingalinga, ding! Ding! Ding!

Stink, Judy, and Opal screeched to a stop. She, Judy Moody, could not believe her eyes. The ice-cream truck had stopped at a red light. Bigfoot was waving his arms, flagging it down. He hopped right onto the ice-cream truck, barely escaping the yowling, howling dogs.

"Did you see that? Bigfoot hijacked the ice-cream truck!" Stink yelled.

"We'll never catch him now," said Judy as the truck pulled away.

"Never say never," said Opal as Jessica Finch rode by on her bike. Opal threw up her hand. "STOP!"

Jessica slammed on her brakes, squealing to a stop.

"I'm afraid we need this bike," said Opal. "It's an emergency."

"Who are YOU?" Jessica Finch asked.

"I'm, uh, Special Agent for the Apprehension of Large Unidentified Creatures. We need this bicycle for the chase."

Stunned, Jessica stepped off her bike.

"Get on!" Opal yelled. Judy hopped on the handlebars; Stink jumped on the back. Pedaling madly, Opal steered the bike across the street, up over the sidewalk, and into someone's front yard, knocking over a yard gnome.

"Woo-hoo!" Judy yelled as they flew through flapping laundry, swerved past a barking dog, and tripped a sprinkler system. *WHOOSH!* A spray of water rained down on them.

"Awesome! No bath tonight!" Stink whooped. Just as they reached the street, they caught sight of the ice-cream truck again.

"We've got him now!" Opal yelled. She poured it on, but the road turned into a steep hill. Huffing and puffing, she stood up on the pedals, groaning with every push. The bike wobbled and swerved.

"Ditch!" Judy yelled, and they all tumbled off the bike. All three of them ran, reaching out for a handhold, but the truck passed them by.

"Back on the bike!" Judy yelled.

Honk. HONK, HONK, HONK! Crr-UNCH! Just then, a van screeched its brakes as its big tires ran over Jessica's bike. The Birnbaums!

"It's Rose and Herb, from my Bigfoot club!" called Stink.

"We got a report! Bigfoot's in—" Herb started.

"—the ice-cream truck. We know!" yelled Stink.

"Get in! Get in!" Herb urged. Opal piled in after Judy and Stink.

"Buckle up, everyone," called Rose taking off like a bat out of Transylvania.

Herb squawked into his CB radio. "This is Herb Birnbaum, reporting a runaway man-gorilla known as Bigfoot who just hijacked an ice-cream truck—"

"LEFT! Go left!" Judy and Stink yelled.

Rose screeched left. "I think I see the truck!" said Opal, pointing.

"Faster!" Judy yelled.

Rose hit the gas. The needle ticked up, up, up. Forty, fifty, sixty . . .

"I have to tell you, this is my first official car chase," said Opal.

"Really? We get in two or three of these a week," said Rose.

"There it is. Right in front of us!" Stink yelled.

All of a sudden, a cloud of ice-cream wrappers flew off the truck, splatting all over the windshield. "It's raining ice cream!" Stink called.

"It's a cloaking device!" Judy said. "Just like in the movies!"

Rose hit the spray and wipers, then punched the gas. Out of nowhere, the WH20 NewsBeat van veered in front of them.

Rose hit the brakes.

"WHOAAAAAAA!" Judy said. "This is like the Scream Monster."

"Minus the puke," Stink teased.

"Follow that van!" Herb ordered.

Rose floored it. She tore down a side

street after the news van, which was zooming after the ice-cream truck. "Shortcut!" she yelled. Rose skidded and bumped crazy-fast across a soccer field.

Ka-bump! Ka-bump! She zoomed through a parking lot full of speed bumps. The van veered out of the lot. Rose zoomed off, still hot on the trail.

The ice-cream truck and news van turned into an old parking lot. The Birnbaums' van roared through a neatly clipped hedge and screeched to a stop.

When the cloud of dust settled, Judy looked around. "Hey, look! It's the Poop Picnic place!"

"Larkspur Pier?" asked Aunt Opal. "How'd that happen?"

Judy and Stink leaped out of the van and raced toward the ice-cream truck.

Hot on their heels were the camera-man and the newscaster. As they got closer, Judy put her finger to her lips. "SHHHHHHH!"

They crept alongside the truck. Judy gasped. "Mr. *TODD?*"

Mr. Todd smiled a big smile when he saw her. "Judy Moody! Long time no see! I was hoping I'd see you —"

"Yeah, because we're saving you from —"

"BIGFOOT!" said Stink.

Bigfoot stepped out of the truck! Everyone gasped. Bigfoot grabbed his head and popped it off.

"ZEKE!" Judy and Stink shrieked at the same time.

Aunt Opal and Rose came running over, all out of breath. Judy and Stink started talking at the same time.

"It's my teacher!"

"It's Zeke!"

"I can't believe he's the ice-cream guy!"

"Since when are you Bigfoot?"

The newscaster waved to the cameraman. "A madcap ride through town has led us to this old pier, where Bigfoot appears to be nothing more than a teenager, wearing some kind of hairy costume!"

Mr. Todd shook hands with Opal. "Hi. Mr. Todd. I'm Judy's teacher, when I'm not being the ice-cream man, that is."

"So *you're* the World's Greatest Teacher," said Aunt Opal. "Nice to meet you finally. I'm Opal Moody. Judy's aunt. When I'm not in pursuit of runaway ice-cream trucks, that is." Everybody cracked up.

"And *this* is Bigfoot," said Mr. Todd. "You all know Zeke. I thought with all the Bigfoot fever around here this summer, it would be fun to get in on the action. I heard about the Bigfoot Club, and went and met Zeke. He came up with a costume, and I hired him to help me sell ice cream today."

"Zeke, why didn't you tell me?" Stink asked.

"Chill, dude! I just got the job. I only met the Todd-ster this morning!"

Judy swatted Stink on the arm. "Stink, why didn't YOU tell ME that Mr. Todd was the ice-cream man? I've been looking for him ALL SUMMER!"

Stink shrugged. "How was I supposed to know?"

The newscaster spoke into the mike. "Today's sightings have been much ado about nothing, but two questions remain. Is the real Bigfoot still at large? And, will he show up for the circus?"

"The circus? Wait! What? Today?" Judy asked.

For the first time, she noticed a huge, striped tent beyond the old Ferris wheel. The pier was all dressed up with banners and balloons.

"Yup! It's today, all right," said Mr. Todd. "And you get a prize for finding me, remember? Front-row seats!"

Judy beamed. "Wow, thanks a million! Was I the first one to find you?"

Mr. Todd's eyes twinkled. "Not exactly . . ."

Opal, Stink, and Judy took their seats in the VIP row, next to a bunch of kids from Judy's class. Judy sat next to Frank Pearl.

"Hey, thanks for getting me a ticket to the circus," Frank said to Judy.

"I owe you," said Judy. "Sorry I was such a fun mop."

"Sponge."

"Mop. Sponge. Rag. Whatever. Want some?" Judy held out her cotton candy to Frank. He made a yuck face.

A hairy gorilla hand grabbed a chunk. "Big-foot hun-gry," said Zeke.

Doo doo doo doo doo doo! A trumpet blared. The ringmaster came onto the stage, leading circus stars atop horses and baby elephants. The kids from circus camp, dressed as clowns, were sweeping up behind the elephants.

"Hey, look—there he is! Rocky!

And he's sweeping ELEPHANT POOP! Ha! I *knew* it!" Judy said. "Hey, Rock! It's me!"

Rocky was dressed in a funny tuxedo and top hat. He waved at Judy. While the clowns did handsprings on the mat, Rocky walked over to a fancy box.

"Do we have a volunteer from the audience?" the ringmaster bellowed. "Someone brave enough to get sawed *in half*?"

Judy was out of her seat in a flash, waggling her arm. Rocky whispered to the ringmaster. He pointed his whip at Judy.

"Yay!" She raced into the ring. Rocky opened the box, motioning her in.

"Hey, Judy!" he said, grinning.

"Hey, Rock. I missed you."

Rocky latched the door. Then he and the ringmaster lifted the box onto sawhorses. Rocky put his saw to the box and started sawing. *ZZZzzzz-ZZZzzzz!*

Abracadabra! She, Judy Moody, was sawed in half. Amazing! Then, *presto change-o,* she was put back together again in no time.

RARE *times two!*

Thrill-a-delic

ᖾ

On a perfect summer evening, a week before school started, when even the mosquitoes weren't biting, Rocky put on a backyard circus for the Moodys. Rocky was wearing his **I WENT TO CIRCUS CAMP** T-shirt, and Amy sported an **I WENT TO BORNEO** tee. Frank had on a **ZOMBIES ARE UNDEAD** shirt.

For the umpteenth time in the last ten days, Rocky said, "And now, before your very eyes, the one and only Judy Moody will be sawed in half."

Judy held up the hand with her mood ring. Blue-green. *Relaxed, Calm.*

"Can I be next?" asked Stink.

Rocky sawed through the middle of the magic box. Judy screamed, kicking her feet wildly. Rocky pushed the two pieces apart until it looked like Judy had been cut in two.

"Ta-da!" said Rocky. Everybody cheered, clapped, and whistled.

"Make sure you put her back!" said Dad.

"Yes," said Mom. "We only just got home!"

"Wow, Rock. That is worth MEGA POINTS!" said Amy.

Rocky pushed the pieces back together. He opened the lid. Judy sat up, in one piece, revealing her handmade **I WENT ON A POOP PICNIC!** T-shirt.

She climbed out of the box. "Don't rub it in, okay? Just 'cause YOU guys beat the pants off me and won the race . . ."

Opal smiled, motioning Judy over. She whispered to Mom and Dad, "Can I borrow Judy for a few minutes? I promise I'll bring her back in ONE piece."

Opal led Judy to the driveway, where she handed her a helmet. They hopped on Zeke's black Vespa and she kick-started the engine with a loud *vroom!* Judy held on to Aunt Opal as they peeled out into the dark night.

"Are you sure you can drive one of these?" Judy asked.

"Duh! I drove one of these across the Sahara! How do you think I got Zeke to let me borrow it?"

Opal zipped through Judy's neighborhood, down Main Street, and turned a corner. Pulling up alongside the Mary Louise Shipman Public Library, she cut the engine. "C'mon," Aunt Opal whispered, stepping off the Vespa. She grabbed a package wrapped in newspaper strapped to the back. "We have to be quick."

Two stern-looking stone lions flanked the front steps. "These guys are WAY too serious, don't you think?" Opal asked. She unwrapped the newspaper and out came the two garbage-can hats, good as new.

"Wow! You fixed them!" Judy cried. She rushed over to place the hats on the lions.

"Yup! Which means you NOW have ... drumroll, please ... TEN thrill points for guerilla art!"

"I did it! FINALLY!" Judy held out her

hand. "Look, Aunt Opal, my mood ring's purple."

"Don't tell me. Purple means *Joyful, On Top of the World.*"

"You knew!"

"Yup. So," Opal said, "it's probably a good thing you didn't spend the summer in your room."

"For sure and absolute positive. I wouldn't have walked on a tightrope, or ridden the Scream Monster, or gone on a scary midnight stakeout . . ."

"Or had a poop picnic," Opal added. Judy and Aunt Opal cracked up.

"OR found Mr. Todd, OR been in a car chase, OR gotten sawed in half at the circus, OR . . . spent the best summer ever . . . with you."

Opal wrapped an arm around Judy as they headed back to the Vespa.

"I have an idea," said Judy. "How about you *don't* leave tomorrow? How 'bout you live with us?"

Aunt Opal gave Judy a hug "I can't. But I'm *so* going to miss you," she told Judy. "You know what, though? *Next* summer, I'm thinking of wrapping the Eiffel Tower in ten thousand scarves. Wanna help me?"

"You mean it? For real? That would be on-top-of-SPAGHETTI rare! Not to mention a gazillion thrill—"

Suddenly, Judy's eyes grew wide. In a sideview mirror of the Vespa, she could see a shaggy, shadowy figure step out of the woods and into a patch of light from a street lamp. Was it? Could it be? Maybe it was just a tall guy with a sweater down to his knees?

Or was it . . . ?

"Aunt Opal!" Judy whispered urgently. "In the mirror! Look! LOOK!"

Aunt Opal peered at the mirror. "I don't see anything. Just the leaves of those bushes are shaking, like somebody just cut through there or something."

"Exactly," Judy half whispered.

The next morning, Judy heard a *toot toot* and looked out the upstairs window. Dad was strapping an enormous suitcase to the top of a taxi.

Judy raced down the stairs as fast as she could. Everybody was hugging and laughing and crying, and Stink was hanging on to Aunt Opal's leg for dear life.

"I'm never letting go," said Stink. Opal climbed into the cab. Stink ran over to the Bigfoot statue.

"Paris. Next summer. Be there!" she

said to Judy. Opal leaned out the window, waving madly, as the cab moved down the street.

"Love you! Bye!" Aunt Opal called.

"Love you back! See you next summer!" Judy sighed and walked over to the Bigfoot statue. Stink was taping a sign onto a card table: TOUCH BIGFOOT! 50 CENTS!

"Fifty cents to touch a piece of shaggy old carpet? Are you nuts?"

"Uh-humm." A throat cleared. "Do you have change for a dollar?"

Judy turned. It was Jessica Finch, on her half-pink bike. The other half was bent, and stickers and glitter covered the scratches. She held out a dollar.

Stink grabbed it. "Sure!"

"Thanks for fixing my bike," said Jessica.

"Yeah, sure, no problem," said Judy.

Stink handed over the change. Jessica slowly stuck out a finger — and touched Bigfoot. "Ewww!" She laughed.

Judy watched as other kids from the neighborhood came down the street. "Fifty cents to touch Bigfoot!" Judy yelled, waving them over.

"Hey! This was MY idea," said Stink.

"Aunt Opal says art belongs to everyone. Besides, I have to earn money for the Eiffel Tower! Fifty cents a touch!" she called, even louder this time. "For a DOLLAR, Bigfoot will shake your hand!

"For a HUNDRED DOLLARS, we'll move him to your yard!" said Dad.

"And for a THOUSAND," said Judy, "I'll show you where the REAL Bigfoot is!"

Judy Moody
and the
NOT Bummer Summer

Based on the characters in the *New York Times* best-selling
Judy Moody children's book series
by Megan McDonald, illustrated by Peter H. Reynolds

"Young actress Jordana
Beatty *is* Judy Moody.
I have to pinch myself
every time I see my
characters leap off the
page and come to life
on the big screen! Rare!"

—Megan McDonald

from Smokewood Entertainment
Screenplay by Kathy Waugh and Megan McDonald
Directed by John Schultz *(Aliens in the Attic)*
Produced by Sarah Siegel-Magness and Gary Magness

SMOKEWOOD
ENTERTAINMENT

Books about Judy:

The Judy Moody Mood Journal

Judy Moody's Double-Rare Way-Not-Boring Book of Fun Stuff to Do

Judy Moody's Way Wacky Uber Awesome Book of More Fun Stuff to Do

Books about Stink:

Stink-O-Pedia: Super Stink-y Stuff from A to Zzzzz

Stink-O-Pedia, Volume Two: More Stink-y Stuff from A to Z

Books about Judy and Stink:

Judy Moody & Stink: The Holly Joliday

Judy Moody & Stink: The Mad, Mad, Mad, Mad Treasure Hunt